About the Author

Ahlam Bsharat is a Palestinian writer who was born in 1975 in the village of Tammun in the Jenin province of Northern Palestine, where she grew up. After completing a Master's Degree in Arabic Literature at An-Najah National University in Nablus, she worked as a teacher for several years, and at present commutes between Tammun and Ramallah, where she works for the Ministry of Culture. Besides poetry, short stories, novels, and memoirs, she has written a number of television and radio scripts.

Bsharat has been active in numerous cultural forums, and her craft has taken her to Belgium and France, where she was artist in residence. She has also led many creative writing workshops for children and adults.

CODE NAME: BUTTERFLY

BY

AHLAM BSHARAT

TRANSLATED FROM THE ARABIC
BY NANCY ROBERTS

Neem Tree
PRESS

Neem Tree Press Limited, 1st Floor,
2 Woodberry Grove, London, N12 0DR, UK

Published by Neem Tree Press Limited 2016
info@neemtreepress.com

Cover design and illustration by Mariam Abbas
Book design by Ghalia Abbas
Edited by Ruth Ahmedzai Kemp

A catalogue record for this book is available from the British Library

ISBN 978-1-911107-02-6 (paperback)
ISBN 978-1-911107-03-3 (e-book)

About the IBBY

The International Board on Books for Young People (IBBY) is a non-profit organisation that was founded in 1953 in Zurich, Switzerland following the destruction of World War II in the belief that books could build bridges of understanding and peace between people.

One of its missions is to bring children and books together by ensuring that books with high literary and artistic standards are available to children everywhere. Books that are windows and books that are mirrors: reflecting ourselves and showing us others.

The IBBY Honour List is a biennial selection of outstanding, recently published books, honouring writers, illustrators and translators from IBBY member countries. The titles are selected by the National Sections of IBBY, who are invited to nominate books characteristic of their country and suitable to recommend for publication in different languages.

Dedication

This book is dedicated to the boys and girls of Palestine.

CONTENTS

CODE NAME: BUTTERFLY

(1)

THE GIGGLES

Baba was dog-tired when he returned from work that day. I could see it in his sun burnt almost blackened face. His brow was knit deep, too, and I sensed the reason was something more than just his job. It wasn't unusual though: my father often entered the house with a grim expression and forbidding air about him, even if he'd just been visiting a friend's house.

Tala and I went silent, like sparrows whose nest is being stalked by a predator under the tree. Not a chirp. Not a breath. But my baby brother Ali wouldn't stop crying.

'He's too little to get scared,' Tala whispered.

She and I were suddenly desperate to crack up laughing, so we clamped our hands over our mouths and scrambled for cover to our room. Honestly, I have no idea why I always needed to giggle uncontrollably whenever things were tense. After Grandpa Abdurrahman—my mother's father—died, for example, I was on edge as soon as I saw his sister, Hajja Safiya, come in through the door. Puffed up like a tent, she tried to cry, but couldn't get a single tear to come out.

As Hajja Safiya wrung her eyes, it happened to start raining outside. The raindrops began pounding against the tinplate sheets that covered the entrance to the front living room. My mother, despite the swollenness of her belly where my brother Ali was comfortably nestled, lumbered to her feet from her cushion on the floor. It seemed Mama wanted to save the day at her own expense, but the weather stepped in for her. It started to rain out of pity for Hajja Safiya, as if the sky thought it might help her shed her own tears.

As I recall, the trigger for my fit of laughter was when Hajja Safiya extended her hand to my mother.

As my mother tried to kiss it, Hajja Safiya deftly drew her hand back as though she'd rehearsed the scene ahead of time. Then she calmly gave it to my mother again so that she could kiss it after all. Mama had a cold and sneezed over Hajja Safiya's extended hand. I suddenly snorted out loud and started giggling—I couldn't help it!

Later that year, when our teacher, Miss Afaf, was helping us rehearse a skit we were performing at the school's year-end assembly, I used Hajja Safiya's hand gesture and the whole funny scene to great comic effect. But on the day of the actual incident I was in very hot water indeed! Hajja Safiya looked daggers at me and, clenching her teeth, labelled me 'ill-bred.' She'd apparently changed her mind about me, since previously she'd always described me as a sensible, well-mannered girl.

My poor mother was mortified as the women in the room suddenly stopped talking to listen to my noisy chortling. Furious, Mama reminded me when we got home that day that this would affect

3

my future.

'What woman would want her son to marry a girl who's got no manners, who opens her mouth and guffaws for the slightest reason, and isn't even sad about her grandfather's death?' she demanded.

Actually, I *was* sad over Grandpa Abdurrahman's death. Those God-awful women—I really detested being around them. When I laughed the way I did that day, they glared at me and started murmuring to each other. They had conveniently forgotten that they themselves had been buzzing away like bees in a hive. *They* were the ones who weren't sad over my grandfather's death. They'd been jabbering on about their husbands and their children, and after pairing up, each couple had started gossiping nastily about the couple just a cushion's throw away. I'd heard them myself. And even when Aunt Bahiya switched on the tape recorder and the room filled with the sound of a sheikh reciting the Qur'an, they went right on chattering!

I pictured their faces—I really couldn't stand any

of them. I thought to myself: *I don't suppose any of them will ever be my mother-in-law. The mother-in-law I have in mind is completely different from all the women in this village. She might be from somewhere else, outside Palestine!*

I used to dream of leaving Palestine, but I never told anyone about it. I didn't expect anybody to understand what it would mean for me even to have a dream! They would have just made fun of me. That's what I assumed, at least. And I especially didn't talk about it with my little sister Tala, since she would have told Mama and all the girls in her class. In fact, Tala would have announced it to everybody she passed in the street the very next morning on her way to school.

I wouldn't have mentioned it to Mays, either, as she would have lectured me about it being wrong for me to want to leave Palestine, 'the land of the sacred bond,' as she put it. So I hid my dream from everybody. I kept it locked away in a safe place—a place you'll find out about soon enough.

The laughing fit I'd experienced during the Hajja Safiya incident happened again in Geography class once, when Maryam had sneaked a bag of crisps into our teacher Miss Nahida's cardigan pocket. She then started extricating a crisp from the bag every time Miss Nahida walked past Maryam's seat. The awful thing was that the bag of crisps kept rustling. We could hear it loud and clear. However, Miss Nahida was not the brightest. She claimed to have eyes in the back of her head but hadn't caught on to the fact that Maryam had been eating crisps under her desk the whole time. In fact, Maryam was even embroidering a rose on a needlepoint canvas at the same time!

So Miss Nahida had absolutely no idea why all of a sudden nobody in the class could keep a straight face. She shrieked. Then she calmed down and threatened to call the principal to the classroom, although she didn't in the end—it wasn't in her best interest. She knew she would be the one looking bad for failing to keep discipline. I felt sorry for her, but I still couldn't stop laughing. She looked at me, crestfallen, and sighed,

'Even the good ones are being silly!'

Anyway, Baba went into the bathroom and, as usual, Mama followed him with the green towel with tree designs on it that got more and more frayed along the edges every time it was used. My mother would snip off the threads that were hanging loose and threaten to throw it away, saying this was the last time Baba would use it. But I knew she wouldn't really carry out her threat, since that would mean having to buy a new one.

My mother wasn't like Uncle Mustafa's wife, who constantly liked to buy new things and tell her neighbours and relatives about every single purchase. It happened so often that everybody concluded the only reason she bought new stuff was to have something to show off about. This was one of the main reasons Uncle Mustafa's wife had such a bad reputation with everybody, especially Grandpa Mubarak and Grandma Amna.

'Girls!' Mama issued her daily summons.

Tala and I just went on giggling silently.

'Girls, fix some food for your father!' Tala mimicked. 'Girls, finish your homework! ... Girls, do your afternoon prayer! ... Girls, come help me stack the vine leaves and cut the stems off!'

Tala's last words came out sounding weary. Panting, she collapsed onto the floor.

'Girls, play with your brother Ali!'

Then we burst out in noiseless hysterics again. We'd given in to the giggles, but we really tried not to make a sound. After all, Tala and I were wimps. We knew what would happen if Baba heard us cracking up at such an awkward time—just when he was tired, hungry and naked in the bathroom, and especially if a thread from the towel got caught on one of his toes or fingers.

Sobering up again suddenly, I barked at Tala, 'That's enough! I'm tired, and so is Baba. We've got to behave ourselves. Besides, you're so skinny, you might throw up if you go on laughing.'

Without really meaning to, I'd managed to make Tala feel nervous and guilty. I'd made it look as though she'd caused the whole ruckus. She dragged herself backwards and, without a word, climbed onto her bed. By this time Ali had stopped bawling, and Baba had finished his shower.

Wearing his old pyjamas, my father sat down cross-legged on the foam mattress with the blue cover on it. He picked up the spoon, which clattered against the bowl as he ate his soup. The tea-kettle boiled over, and as it hissed and spluttered, I heard my mother run over, muttering, to turn off the gas.

Some time in the middle of the afternoon, we gathered around a huge pile of vine leaves. Ever since I'd opened my eyes to the world, our house had been filled with them. When I was a toddler I would play with the leaves until somebody took them away from me, or me away from them. When I was a bit older, my mother would call me to come and help her prepare them. First she would have me stack them in neat piles. Then she started to let me take off the stems. At first I did it with my teeth. Running my tongue over my lips, I'd pick up what remained of the sour flavour until my throat was dry and I had a bitter taste in my mouth. Sometimes I'd snap them off with my fingernails, which would turn the nails blackish green. The next day I'd have to try all sorts of ways to hide my hands from my classmates, and especially from Haya, who was even more pompous and sanctimonious than Hajja Safiya, or Mama for that matter when she was pregnant with Ali. So I pestered my mother to let me use the knife, and in the end, she did.

At first she stipulated that I use the serrated paring knife. She also made me sit in the corner so I wouldn't hurt any of my brothers or sisters with the sharp tip. The first time I got to use the paring knife to remove the vine leaf stems, I was in seventh heaven. I felt as though I'd grown up all of a sudden, and that meant I'd be able to understand my sister Zaynab. It seemed as though Zaynab's world was full of secrets, some of which she shared with my mother.

For example, she would get a stomach ache, and my mother would pile blankets on top of her. She'd make her an infusion of sage and fenugreek in a small pot, and then set it next to her head with her big mug. I wished I had a mug like that. Mama would send my brother Abdullah to the corner shop, and he'd come back with three yellow packages inside a black bag. Each of the yellow packages had a picture of a smiling baby on it.

I would wonder what Zaynab had to do with smiling babies. Deep down I'd feel really uneasy, because maybe babies had something vaguely to do with a person's honour, and judging from the way I'd heard my mother and everybody else talk about it, honour was a dangerous matter!

I continued feeling anxious about it until my mother started piling blankets on top of me, too, making me sage and fenugreek infusions and pouring them into a big glass, since I didn't have a mug like Zaynab's. The mystery had been solved, although the packages were a different colour now and didn't have pictures of smiling babies on them, as a different company made them. Or maybe it was just that, since Zaynab had become an expert on such things, she preferred other brands now, like the ones we saw advertised on television.

After a while I started to get bored of cutting off vine leaf stems, even if I did get to do it with a serrated knife. It was the first time I began to feel that, perhaps, growing up wasn't so amazing after all. I started trying to wheedle out of the chore, using tests, homework or other housework for excuses. I'd say I needed to do the washing up after lunch, for example, even though I hated washing dishes.

My mother, of course, always knew how to outmanoeuvre me, especially when my brothers and sisters objected to my tricks. She would find some other chore for me instead, like packing the leaves into bags, weighing them and arranging them neatly somewhere out of my younger siblings' reach. Then I'd have to sit and guard the bags as I opened my history book. My homework that day might be on something like the massacres that were committed as part of the occupation of Palestine, for example, so that in addition to having to count and guard the bags of vine leaves, I'd also have to memorise all sorts of awful dates and statistics.

I didn't understand at first what it meant for Baba to work in an Israeli settlement. He planted and looked after the grapevines. He also worked as a driver and would transport labourers from our village and neighbouring villages to the settlement to pick grapes and vine leaves and to prune the vines. He would sell the produce and hand over the money he'd earned to Gabby, an Israeli settler.

My father was completely devoted to his job, as though he were working on land he owned himself, rather than land the Israelis had seized from him and his ancestors. At the same time, he packed me off to school to get an education. There I had to memorise the dates of the massacres the occupiers had committed against us. I would take tests on it all and get good grades.

When I was old enough to start questioning all this, I didn't dare ask Baba anything. So I decided to keep my questions hidden away in the same place where I hid the dreams I couldn't confide in anyone for fear that they would make fun of me.

I remembered how Haya and Mays had said that my father was working in a settlement for occupiers who were killing our people. They were the ones who had murdered my Uncle Saleh as he was driving people to Nablus in his car. They'd ordered him to get out of the car and then turn around. So he'd turned around, and they shot him over and over in the back. That's how my little cousin Salem lost his father.

They had even left mines in the mountains around our village. One had gone off under Bakr, who lost both his legs. After that, Bakr just sat in bed all day propped up with pillows, or crawled on the floor even though he was my age. He had eyes as green as a wheat field. I didn't understand, but I didn't dare ask Baba about it. I didn't get the giggles, either. Instead I just felt miserable, and kept my question about it hidden carefully away.

My father took some sweets out of his pocket one day. He said they were from Gabby's wife. When it was my turn—by which time there was only one sweet left—I lied, saying, 'I've got a tummy ache.'

I felt as though Haya and Mays were watching me, and I was sure they would make some sarcastic comment about me eating sweets sent to us by an occupier's wife. Tala became all excited and insisted the sweet was hers, then, since I didn't want it. When Munir complained that he should get it because he was the youngest, Tala's retort was that since she and I were both girls, it should go to her.

They went on fighting like this until Baba dealt with their argument by taking the sweet and shoving it back in his pocket, saying he'd save it for one of the workers he took to the settlement, or give it to our little cousin Abboud if he saw him. ('Abboud' was the nickname of my Uncle Mustafa's little boy

Abd as-Samad.) Or, he said in an afterthought, he might give it to my sister Zaynab when she came home from the university that evening.

I was thinking about the different comments Haya and Mays always made. Mays was a nationalist, which justified the kinds of things she said and made it easier for me to put up with them. But all Haya cared about was her eyebrows and her fingernails. Even though the teacher had threatened to report her more than once, she just went right on plucking her eyebrows and pencilling them in, and growing her fingernails long. When the teacher told Haya she'd have her mother come to the school, Haya agreed, nodding with a smirk across her face.

After the teacher had left, she told us it was her mother who encouraged her to do these things, since all the girls in her extended family in Nablus pencilled their eyebrows and painted their fingernails. She said they called her a country bumpkin when she went to visit family over the holidays.

'But if I manicure my nails and pencil my

eyebrows into arches, they won't treat me like I'm not one of them!'

She seemed depressed when she said that, and not quite herself, as if in a dilemma. However, moods like this normally didn't last more than a few minutes with her. But what I couldn't understand was why she always went on about Palestinian patriotism and yet forgot about her grandfather, who was rumoured to be an informer for the Israelis.

It was my mother who had told me about Haya's grandfather being an informer. The occupiers would turn up at his house in their jeeps. Then, when some young men in balaclavas tried to interrogate him, he fled to Israel, and he remained there from the time of the first Intifada. Being his only son, Haya's father used to visit him regularly in Israel after he fled. Haya's father received a lot of money from him, and who knows? Maybe he provided her grandfather with important news about the village in return for it.

After telling me these things, my mother blew

into the neck opening of her loose-fitting tunic and muttered, and I understood. This was something both my mother and Grandma Amna used to do whenever they repeated hearsay. Rumours that Haya's father was a collaborator like his own father weren't necessarily true. After all, Haya's father—who used to sit by the window in his little shop where he sold *Siniora* processed meat, cans of tuna, sacks of flour, mobile phone credit for both *Al Jawwal* and *Cellcom* sim cards—seemed like a respectable man. So my mother made me promise to keep my mouth shut. What she'd told me was a kind of secret, and if it hadn't been for my constant moaning about Haya's jibes regarding Baba's work, she wouldn't have mentioned anything to me about it. She might have felt sorry for me too, since I'd started to cry as I was complaining to her about Haya.

On the other hand, maybe my mother wasn't as sympathetic as I'd imagined. And maybe it was wrong of me to extract her secret by emotional manipulation. Maybe I was being 'shrewd' as

I remember people describing me sometimes, although I never knew exactly what they meant by it.

Sometimes I thought the word 'shrewd' meant 'resourceful' or 'perceptive'. At other times people seemed to use the word with negative connotations. For example, they might imply it meant 'dishonest', which wasn't true of me at all. I assumed that in regard to the things my mother had told me about Haya's father, I was just being perceptive.

And that's how everyone ought to see it! I told myself.

In any case, it wasn't as if I had any intention of blackmailing Haya with this piece of information. After all, she was my friend, although people tended to think that was a bit strange. She was Mays's friend, too, which especially surprised the teachers. As Umm Badr, the school's cleaning lady put it, Haya, Mays and I were 'a motley crew', and whenever she saw us together she would quote her favourite Arabic proverb:

'What would bring a *Shami* together with a *Maghrebi*?'

It was true, of course, that Haya and I were friends. But I knew the day would come when we'd have a falling out, the way everybody does sooner or later. And that meant I might need that crucial piece of information at some point in the future. When exactly, I didn't know. I wasn't going to sit around waiting for it. But the day was surely coming, and I needed to be prepared.

(2)

THE STORY OF
THE EYEBROWS

Summer rolled around fast. Now that the grape season was over, Baba went to work picking dates for the same settlement. Only this time he was on Yuval's farm.

'The dates need special care, or they'll go bad,' Baba used to say.

He provided the requisite care with such complete dedication, in fact, that one day he tore a muscle in his right leg. My father was unfailingly honest in his work, and whenever he saw my brothers, my sisters, my mother or me busy with some task, he loved to quote a saying of the Prophet (peace and blessings be upon him) that goes,

'It pleases God that if you do a job, you do it

with perfection.'

One day Tala was colouring in a picture she'd drawn for her art class at school. Munir was doing his maths homework. I was practising writing some new English words in my exercise book. And my mother was folding clean laundry on the big chair with Ali dangling from one of her full breasts.

As my father recited his beloved quotation, Munir's and Tala's heads came together all of a sudden as if they were tied to a thread that was being pulled upward by an invisible hand. Grinning to myself, I could hear them whispering, bursting with giggles.

'So, Baba,' I said jokingly, 'do you think we're workers ready to pick grapes or dates for you?'

At first my father tried to appear angry, but he couldn't disguise the fact that he appreciated my question. I'd been making an obvious, and deliberate, reference to the fact that he had a position of authority in his job, and that he had workers who took orders from him. His face flushed with a mixture of irritation and pride.

'Ahem,' he cleared his throat, as he usually did, and as I'd known he would.

My mother smiled, glad to see that, contrary to what Uncle Mustafa's wife would have liked, her family was getting along just fine.

I thought back on a few things Mays and Haya had said and, with a mixture of sadness and intuition, I thought to myself: *You're nothing but a labourer yourself, Baba. Gabby and Yuval are the real bosses, and they'd fire you in a minute if you made the slightest mistake, even over something as teeny tiny as baby Ali's shoes!*

Of course, I wouldn't have wanted my father to go against what the Prophet (peace and blessings be upon him) had said about doing your work perfectly, or for him to betray Gabby and Yuval. At the same time, though, there was something I couldn't quite understand. When we asked our religious studies teacher at school *if it was all right to steal from the occupiers,* she told us it was wrong. Mays and I weren't totally convinced, though.

We got into a complete muddle as we talked about it on the way home from school one day. As if she wanted an explanation to justify our confusion, Mays said, 'Maybe we can't think straight because we're getting sun stroke in this terrible heat. Or maybe it's because we're exhausted from walking so much, or because we're starving!'

I'd always envied Mays, assuming she knew everything. However, I wasn't persuaded by her theories this time. I concluded that she didn't know as much as I'd always thought she did, and all of a sudden I felt the need for real answers. I let out a frustrated groan, and Haya, who had been walking nearby with Sawsan and giving her the latest scoop on the star of the soap opera they were both besotted with, glanced in my direction.

Sneering, she said to me, 'You shouldn't worry about politics. After all, Palestine will never be liberated no matter what you do.'

Even more furious now, I grabbed Haya by the

hair. I thought of saying, *'Yeah. It'll never be liberated as long as your father and your grandfather trot our news over to the enemy!'* But I was astute enough to catch myself, and what came out instead was, 'Yeah, as long you go on pencilling your eyebrows into arches!'

I was hungry and tired, and the sun was blazing. So I convinced myself that the reasons Mays had suggested for why we couldn't make sense of it all were good enough for the time being, at least. The last thing I needed was to go home feeling even worse than usual.

If I got into a serious fight with Haya, I wouldn't be able to eat lunch, since she was my friend, after all, and I'd get upset whether I wanted to or not. And if I didn't eat, I'd just end up curling up in bed and crying, which would mean not studying for my grammar test, and I really needed to improve my grade.

My parents might not have been too worried about our grades most of the time, but on the other hand, sometimes—like in the middle of the semester, or at the end of the school year—they'd suddenly remember they had children in school and would start showing an interest in our grades.

So I'd always try and remind myself what it felt like to stand in front of Baba to show him my report card, or to eavesdrop on Mama and Baba as he asked her about our grades in school. Tala and I would either crowd up against the door, or jump into bed and bury ourselves under the covers—depending, of course, on whether our grades had been good or bad. Sometimes Tala would stand up proud as a little peacock as she handed my father a test paper she'd done especially well on. And I suppose I did the same, the only difference being that I was a taller and skinnier peacock.

In any case, Mays intervened between Haya and me, and the squabble didn't go beyond Palestine's freedom and Haya's eyebrows. It could have been worse, and I went home more or less satisfied with the way the day had gone. Even so, I decided to hide another question in my treasure chest—the little box where I locked away questions I hadn't found answers to, or that I was too afraid to ask. It was also where I buried the secret dreams I suspected other people would make fun of for one reason or another. Nobody had an inkling about my questions, my dreams, or the treasure chest—not even Tala—and I wouldn't have told her about them even if she'd sworn herself to secrecy a thousand times on her Qur'an with the zip-up cover.

That evening I found myself alone in the room I shared with Tala and Zaynab. I stepped over to the window and gazed at the sun as it set, leaving the remains of its crimson robe on the hilltop. I loved the sight. I looked down toward the foot of the hill, which was where my father worked on an Israeli settlement. The settlement was neat and tidy, like the towns you see in cartoons. The houses with their red terracotta roof tiles were all the same size and the same distance apart, with green trees all around them. They were beautiful, and yet I didn't like them at all—they made me feel scared.

I settled down cross-legged on the bed and closed my eyes, picturing a beautiful, big city that was ours, not theirs. I'd always liked to draw cities and houses in my imagination. I'd fill them with whomever I wanted. I'd bring to life anybody I wanted, and kill whomever I wanted. I wanted to create a city that belonged just to us, and that they had no share in at all. They would have none of the date palms and grapevines. There would be no labourers or any settlements like the ones Baba had to work in. Then Mays and Haya wouldn't have any excuses for making sarcastic comments about his job.

I thought about the last thing Mays had told me as we were on our way home from school. She'd said, 'My uncle used to be a construction worker in Israel. Then one day he fell off the fourth floor and broke his spine, but his boss refused to acknowledge him because he'd been working there without a permit.' I started thinking about my father, and a shudder of fear went through me, though at the time I didn't know why.

Baba had a work permit, and he had to go every few months to get it stamped at the Civil Administration office in Huwwara. He'd leave very early in the morning and get back extremely late, and he always came home looking irritated for some reason, even when he'd got the stamp he needed. Tala and Munir would race to meet him and, without even a glance at his face, they'd grab the bags he was carrying out of his hands. Then they would open them up, eager to gobble down whatever delicious treats they found inside. But they'd burst into tears if they didn't find their beloved harisa, and they'd leave the bags strewn on the ground, for Baba to pick up again and bring the rest of the way in.

When I looked into his face, I would read things I couldn't fathom, and which I didn't dare ask him about. My father was never harsh or mean, but I wasn't comfortable asking him the questions in my head. Instead I'd hole up in my room and sit on my bed, squirrelling away my questions and ignoring the antics Tala always used to try and distract me or to make sense of my secret rituals.

Now that we were in the summer season, villagers would come knocking on our door to ask my father to help them get jobs. They'd bring their ID cards in the hope of getting work permits from the Civil Administration, which only issued them to people whose records showed that they weren't suspected of any attempts to breach Israeli security.

Most of the job seekers were school boys, but some were university students or graduates. Even Mays's brother came to ask my father about work, which came as a surprise to me. Mays often criticised my father's job, and her brother Muhammad was locked up, serving the first of three consecutive life sentences. *So why would her other brother want to work for the Israelis?*

I considered calling Mays to ask her about it myself, too impatient to wait until the next morning. But if I did, my mother was sure to eavesdrop on the conversation the way she always did when I called my friends or answered the phone. I hated this habit of hers, especially since Zaynab had her own phone and could make and receive calls whenever she wanted to. She could even do it surreptitiously in the middle of the night, from under the covers. So I didn't phone Mays. If nothing else, my mother would probably have thought it was a silly question for me to ask. Or she might think it was some sort of secret coded language meant to camouflage something else.

I wouldn't have put it past her to ask, the way Haya had, 'Since when are you interested in politics?' Only, instead of adding, 'You shouldn't worry about it. Palestine will never be liberated anyway,' my mother would have said, 'Do you want to end up like your Uncle Yasin?' If she had said that, she wouldn't, of course, have been ridiculing my Uncle Yasin, who died a martyr. But she would have been ridiculing me. Knowing this, I concluded it was best to hide the question away in the treasure chest along with all the others. I was in no mood to have a row with my mother.

From the minute I realised how soon the summer holidays were starting, a strange kind of melancholy came over me. Once school was out, I wouldn't be able to leave the house anymore unless it was some special occasion, and I'd have to get my father's official permission. Zaynab also seemed to be in an especially bad mood around that time.

Sometimes she would cry at night. I would hear her sobs coming from under the blanket, soft and muffled. When the sobbing became louder I'd hold my breath so she wouldn't realise I could hear her and be embarrassed. Whenever Tala stirred and nudged me, half asleep, to pass her a drink, since our beds were right next to each other, I'd clear my throat the way Baba did sometimes. I used to rehearse it on the odd occasion that Tala and I were home alone together, and I made use of it at night as a way of indirectly signalling to Zaynab to get ready to stop crying so Tala wouldn't hear her and tell Mama.

Tala and I had quite a few silly little secrets in common, because we tended to get into mischief together. Every time I had a new secret plan I'd swear I wasn't going to let her in on it. But then she'd start begging and pleading. I'd make her promise she wasn't going to open her mouth again no matter what, and she would run to get her little Qur'an with the zip. Then, her hand shaking, she would open it up and swear on it. As she took her oath her lips would quiver, and she looked hilarious and pitiful at the same time.

One time Tala swore on her Qur'an like this when I needed her to keep quiet about trying out Mama's make-up. I couldn't help chuckling, but fortunately she didn't see. She had her head bowed, with a beseeching, helpless look on her face. I held my hand over my mouth to stifle a loud hoot, and my cheeks puffed up. Finally I opened my mouth a crack, and it made a hissing sound like when air seeps out of a balloon.

About a week after that, when Mama asked what we'd done with a stick of lipstick that had disappeared, Tala kept quiet, acting as good as gold. But not long afterwards, despite me eyeing her ferociously, she decided to own up.

'Oh, all right! I lost it!' she cried. After a fitful sigh, she added, 'We both used it. Then when we went to wash off our faces, it fell out of my hand into the sink and dissolved in the water. But I didn't use it because I wanted to, Mama. She told me to!'

With this final addition, she pointed at me with a steady hand. Surprised at this sudden show of strength, I glared at her out of one eye while trying to keep the eye nearest my mother closed in the hope of looking sorry. At a moment like that I didn't want to come across as 'shrewd', since it might have prompted my mother to punish us more severely. Perhaps the strategy worked, because the storm passed. All my mother did was scold me and say, 'Well, it's only natural that you'd do something like that under Haya's influence. This is the end of your friendship with that girl, you hear?'

She swore she was going to come to the school to make sure I'd broken things off with Haya. I knew, of course, that she wouldn't actually come to the school and that I wouldn't really have to stop being friends with Haya. But at the time it all seemed real enough. I had to play along and keep to the script. I even cried, with some little tears dripping down the sides of my nose onto my lips. I decided to taste my tears, and they were so salty that I screwed up my face. In the end I headed for the kitchen and started washing dishes as calmly as I could. Any nervous movement might mean a broken plate or glass, which would have meant God knows what punishment.

As I disappeared behind the kitchen door, Tala was standing across from me. I stuck my tongue out at her and shook my fist as a sign that I wouldn't forget her betrayal. For a second she shrank like a mouse. But then she tossed her hair back coolly in a show of indifference.

Not long after that, wanting to be the perfect big sister, I decided to show leniency, as grown-ups used to say, and give Tala another chance. When everybody else was out, I swore her to secrecy again. As proof of her good intentions, I asked her to sit outside and guard the front door, and to give me a quick signal if she saw anybody coming. She was curious about what I was going to do, but I told her that if she asked questions, I wouldn't be able to trust her promise. She proclaimed that according to her school teacher, 'oaths were sacred'. She said this thinking that she could twist my arm into telling her what I was up to, but I outsmarted her. I informed her that this was a way of testing to see how sincere her promise actually was, and that the next time I might just guard the front door myself.

It felt good to try on my mother's red nightgown. It was huge on me, of course, but I pinned it in the back to make it fit. I looked pretty, like the backing singers on television. I let my hair down around my shoulders then pulled it back. My face, my neck and my eyes looked downright captivating—I was even more gorgeous than Haya now!

I ran my hands over my little breasts. I wished they would grow, since all my attempts to make them look bigger had been a total flop. I opened Zaynab's drawer, put on one of her bras, and started stuffing the cups with paper tissues until they seemed big enough to me. Haya wasn't embarrassed to talk about her breasts and other things that my mother had drilled into me were shameful to mention. Haya was dying to get to the lesson at school on the reproductive system, and she'd leaf ahead in the textbook and count how many pages we had left before we got there. I couldn't wait either and in the middle of the night when I was worried and couldn't sleep, I'd think about the things I'd been reading from our Science book on the sly.

When the day finally came for the long-anticipated lesson, the whole class was buzzing. Even though our science teacher tried to be more serious than ever, you could see a cryptic smile glimmering through her sombre features. With an audacity that, I must say, impressed me—though I never admitted it to her—Haya asked, 'Do the sperm come out with the urine?' The teacher answered her question in the negative and went on to the next point without any additional explanation. Then Haya interrupted with another question about why millions of sperm are produced even though it only takes one to fertilise an egg. It really was puzzling to think about.

On our way home from school, I tried to pose a question that would be as puzzling as Haya's, though I did it in a very matter-of-fact way so as not to let on to her that I didn't know much about the reproductive system. She saw through me, of course, and laughed her head off. I would have had a hard time extricating myself from the situation if it hadn't been for Mays's intervention.

My question was how the sperm and the egg got together if they started out in separate bodies. What was so funny about that? But funny or not, Haya pounced on my question and used it as an excuse to crack up whenever she felt like it. She kept on repeating the word 'separate' as though it was the punch line to some hilarious joke. Things went on this way for days until I started seeing the word 'SEPARATE' stamped on Haya's face every time I looked at her. As a result, the reproductive system took its own place in my treasure chest, but along with memories of a different flavour—tinged with desire, fear and hostility.

I examined my breasts in the mirror. They looked quite big now. The tissue I'd stuffed into the bra cups had saved me the extra time I would have needed to fill out naturally. Then I peered at my face and noticed what bushy eyebrows I had.

Suddenly it occurred to me that if I plucked them just a little bit, nobody would notice. If I did it just occasionally, then little by little I'd get used to my new look, and so would my mother and everybody else. Maybe that was what Zaynab had done at first, and my mother, too. After all, both of them plucked their eyebrows without worrying about what anyone might say. *So why was it all right for them and my teachers Miss Nahida and Miss Fayrouz to pluck their eyebrows, but not for Haya and me?*

It was a question worth asking, so I hid it in my treasure chest, too. It also made me feel justified in doing what I wanted to with my eyebrows. I have to confess, though—my hand was shaking. Every now and then I'd open the door and spy on Tala to make sure she was still doing her job right. Sometimes I'd find her playing with the cat, Wadee, and other times she'd be playing with a ball. Reassured, I'd try to go back to work with a steadier hand.

When everybody arrived home later, the first being my mother, everything seemed normal. To be on the safe side, I put on a brown headscarf and drew it down over my forehead. But I could tell my eyebrows didn't look any different, since there was no comment about them from Haya, Mays or any of the other girls at school the next day.

So it seemed that I was the only one living through the saga of my eyebrows. Apart from that, everything seemed to be business as usual. My father came home from work exhausted. Zaynab helped my mother make pastries with the spinach and chard Baba had brought from the settlement, before going to bed and crying herself to sleep under the covers.

Even though Haya hadn't done very well on the maths test that day, it didn't stop her blabbering away merrily about her favourite soap opera characters the whole way home from school. And Mays had tried to bring up the subject of whether it was all right to steal from the occupiers so that we could broaden our options, but I really wasn't in the mood to discuss it with her.

This was before I'd reached home to discover that nothing had changed since I'd plucked a few hairs out of my eyebrows, so I was still a little tense. Noticing how I was feeling, Mays made small talk, remarking that the sun wasn't as hot as it had been the day before. As she was busy chattering, I ran my hands over my breasts. They were still puny—the way they always were without padding, I sighed to myself.

(3)

CODE NAME: BUTTERFLY

One evening I was sitting on my bed. Tala was jumping up and down on hers making an obnoxious creaking noise. She was jabbering away, but I wasn't taking in anything she was telling me since I was preoccupied with the city I was building in my head. Then she started dashing in and out of the room, and every time she came back in, I was in the same trance as before.

Finally, though, as she hurried back in I heard the sound of a little boy crying. It was my cousin Salem. The minute I saw him, I rushed over to my schoolbag and pulled out a piece of chocolate I'd been planning to eat after Tala and Munir went to sleep. Still crying, Salem started munching on the chocolate. Tears streaming down his face and his nose running, he asked, 'Why is Uncle Rashid going to be sleeping in Baba's bed?'

I felt like bursting into tears too, but it didn't seem like the right time, since I needed to look after Salem. Instead, I ran to grab a tissue to wipe his face before the chocolate got all mixed up with his tears and the snot slithering from his nose.

Speaking to him the way adults talk to children when they haven't got all the facts, I said, 'Let's you and I hide this question in my treasure chest, as I don't really know the answer to that right now.'

Calmer now, he stopped eating. 'Where is it?' he asked with interest. It was the first time I'd been asked where the treasure chest was. I could hear Tala meowing along with Wadee outside.

'Come over here!' I said to him.

We scrambled to the floor and I told him it was under my bed, where nobody would expect to find it.

As we lay there crammed under the bed, he whispered, 'Is it under the tiles?'

He'd spared me having to think up more answers that might seem far-fetched and unconvincing. 'Exactly,' I said. 'It's under the tiles. And I keep the key with Grandma Amna in the tents all the way on the outskirts of the village.'

I'd been expecting him to ask me about the key, so I knew I needed to think of some hiding place that was a long way away, and as far as Salem was concerned, the tented camp where Grandma Amna and Grandpa Mubarak lived was about as far away as you could get—at the end of the world.

Salem's face looked tiny and pale, and the corners of his mouth were covered in chocolate.

'Couldn't the army go there and steal it?' he asked fearfully.

'Absolutely not,' I assured him, puffing out my cheeks. I furrowed my brow and continued, 'And even if they did go there, they wouldn't be able to find the key, since Grandma Amna has lots of secret hiding places.'

He went quiet for a little while as he busied

himself licking the chocolate wrapper.

'So,' he asked, worried again, 'who'll answer the questions that are under the tiles?'

I scratched my head. Then, trying not to come across as uncertain as I felt, I said, 'God will!'

Taking his hand as I slid out from under the bed, I added, 'God knows things we don't. He's the only one that knows where your Baba and all the other martyrs have gone.'

He scooted back and leaned against the side of the bed. He seemed to accept my explanation, and had forgotten all about crying.

Then he declared with adult-like confidence, 'Yes, and God has heaven—a big garden that's full of bananas and apples. Baba's living in a castle there, and he's waiting for me to grow up and come visit him.'

His words came out in a steady rush with him hardly taking a breath. I nodded, and couldn't help starting to cry myself. To keep Salem from noticing, I took him into my arms and held him close. But I guess I squeezed a little too hard, since he started trying to wriggle out of my grasp. Saying he wanted to go out and look for Wadee, he slipped impishly away, and I sat there by myself, drying my tears.

After he was gone I added another question to my treasure chest: *Why has Salem grown up so fast?*

I also couldn't understand why Rashid was marrying Salma, who'd been married to his brother Saleh until he'd died about a year before. But I heard my mother tell our neighbour, Umm Ali, 'It's only natural. He's got to protect his brother's honour and take care of his flesh and blood.'

It terrified me to hear the words 'honour' and 'flesh' in the same sentence. The word 'honour' was one that people used a lot in our village, and when they did, they talked in a strange way, as if losing it was some sort of catastrophe, like the Israeli occupation.

My mother used the word a lot, especially when she talked about my relationship with Haya. Sometimes I'd even have nightmares about our friendship causing me a problem relating to my honour, and, more specifically, my breasts, and it would remind me of the Biology lesson on the reproductive system. For example, I might dream that Haya had found out I was obsessed with waiting for Nizar to walk by our house, that I would stand on tiptoe to see him, or that I'd thought more than once of writing him a note (I only thought about it, though). I'd also bought him a present once—a bottle of cheap cologne—with a card that had a picture of two little children hugging on it. But I'd never actually given it to him—it was still in my drawer, and every time Tala tried to open the drawer, I'd pick a fight with her.

I wondered if Haya could get inside my head and read my thoughts. She could in my nightmares, which always revolved around the word 'honour'. I would wake up in a panic, feeling as though I had barely slept and that the night had flashed past too quickly. That's when I wished there could be a special day off school for children who couldn't sleep because of their nightmares. It happens to Palestinian kids all the time. Of course, I couldn't possibly have asked for a 'Nightmare Day Off', because everybody would have made fun of me— even the school counsellor. So I decided to hide the idea in my precious little treasure chest.

Rashid was five years younger than Salma, and if I hadn't been crazy about Nizar, who was so gorgeous, especially when he wore his black trousers and his silvery grey sweater in the winter, I might have thought of Rashid as the man of my dreams, since he was really handsome, with dimples in both cheeks, and he trimmed his beard so elegantly.

I liked Rashid's beard, but not Uncle Mustafa's. His was long and bushy, and it scratched my face when he kissed me on *Eid Al Adha*. Uncle Mustafa grew his beard long for religious reasons. He said it was a way of following the Sunnah, or example of the Prophet Muhammed (peace and blessings be upon him). But there were lots of things about Uncle Mustafa that I didn't like and that I thought he should change. At the very least, I thought he should get his wife to stop being such a compulsive shopper. But I didn't bring it up with him. Instead I just hid this question too in my treasure chest and asked him something else: 'Uncle Mustafa,' I said, 'don't you have a razor?'

When I said this, he laughed, and so did my father and Grandpa Mubarak. But Uncle Mustafa's laugh was my favourite, because he had a gold tooth that twinkled like a star at the end of a witch's magic wand.

Emboldened by their reaction, I asked him, 'And why doesn't Grandpa Mubarak grow a beard?'

Grandpa Mubarak was religious, too, and Grandma Amna was no spendthrift, but Grandpa had been clean-shaven for as long as I could remember. In any case, Grandpa Mubarak, my father and Uncle Mustafa all laughed, but none of them answered my question. *Did they think I'd just cracked a joke?!*

While Rashid was handsome, Salma wasn't ugly,

but she wasn't pretty either. I'd never been able to decide whether she enjoyed life or not. However, it had been easy to see that she was depressed when her husband Saleh was martyred. Before that she had been somewhere in the middle, just like everybody else. She didn't laugh, but she would smile at least, and she cared a lot about her appearance. Sometimes when I bumped into her going somewhere, I'd notice she was wearing eyeliner and lipstick. I remember admiring the colour of the lipstick she was wearing the last time I saw her before Saleh was killed. I still recall the colour clearly, though I don't know why I recall that one thing in particular. But I often do that, of course, remembering some things and forgetting others, and the details I remember aren't necessarily the most important ones.

On Salma and Rashid's wedding day, Salem was miserable. But he did get the chocolate, at least. My mother might have sent him to me knowing I'd find a way to cheer him up. She trusted me, I think, even though she never said so straight out.

Salem wanted to play with Wadee, so I told my mother I'd stay home with him instead of going to the wedding. I didn't have anything to do in the house and was bored out of my mind, but I was glad not to go—I'd had a feeling I'd be upset if I went, not to mention the fact that for some reason or another I didn't approve of this wedding, which nobody but Salem had consulted me about.

The other reason for my not going was that I didn't want to miss the chance to see Nizar pass by on his way home from the university. I always kept an eye out for him, and since he'd gone out, he was bound to be coming home again. I also thought maybe he'd give me some sign—something more significant than just looking at me and smiling the way he usually did.

That summer things got to the point where the whole of my existence revolved around waiting for Nizar to pass by, and I tracked his every move. There was nothing more important in life. When the school holidays began, I didn't get to chat with Haya and Mays anymore, and the only thing on television was bad news. In the mornings, Munir and Tala would take it over to watch children's programmes on Channel 3, and in the afternoons my mother would watch her depressing soap operas. Noticing how tense she was all the time, Zaynab and I would say to her,

'As if we needed any more tragedies around here! Isn't it enough that we Palestinians keep fighting both the occupation and each other?'

To be honest, I should mention that it was Zaynab who did most of the talking. All I did was try to support her by nodding or repeating some of what she'd said. Then 'Miss Tala' would start making fun of me. 'Parrot!' she would giggle, and an argument would break out between us. At the same time, though, I could understand my mother's point of view. After all, the misery she saw on the Arabic TV channels gave her a kind of break from her own worries.

'Thank you, O Arabic Channels, for offering

us such consolation!' Zaynab and I would chant sarcastically.

In the evenings it was Baba's turn to monopolise the television. He'd watch the news on a Hebrew channel, and on the Arabic *Al Arabiya* and *Al Jazeera*, but he never listened to the various 'Palestinian factions', as he referred to them. I was dying to ask him why he listened to everybody but the Palestinians, and why he even swore at them sometimes.

But I never did. Instead, I hid the question away in my treasure chest along with another one: *Is Baba siding with the occupation the way Haya and Mays want me to believe? In other words, is my father like Haya's father and grandfather?*

As time went on, the questions nearly overwhelmed me. I felt as though my head, and my treasure chest, were about to explode. When I tried to give my mother an idea of what was going on in my head, she told me I shouldn't dwell on such things. As she put it, 'Things have always been hard, and we don't want to make them worse. But if everybody starts gossiping and bickering without weighing their words, there'll be fighting and arguments all over the place, and that will just make the occupiers happy.'

So as not to 'make the occupiers happy', I'd have to make my treasure chest even bigger so that I could stuff all my questions into it. I even started thinking that I might be able to fit into it myself. As time went on, I liked the idea more and more, so I started looking up facts about cocoons. My treasure chest was like a cocoon that would let me turn from a caterpillar into a colourful butterfly. And then I could fly high up in the sky.

After all, I thought, maybe people are hatched from questions the way chickens and bugs are hatched from eggs and larvae. It seemed like such a strange idea that my head nearly exploded.

But all these ideas helped me see my treasure chest in new ways. At first it had just been a safe place to hide questions and dreams, and it had ended up as an incubator for a butterfly. The butterfly was my favourite symbol now, and I thought about the possibility of naming my daughter 'Butterfly' some day.

But I knew it wouldn't be acceptable, so I decided instead to use it as my alter ego. That way I'd have a code name like Mays, who called herself Dalal after the martyred Palestinian freedom-fighter Dalal Mughrabi, and like Fida, a girl in another class whose classmates called her al-Khansa after the Arabian poetess, because like the poetess, Fida had two brothers who'd been martyred: Samir, who'd died in the first Intifada, and Fadi, who'd died in the second. Her brother Mazin was in prison, and on top of that, the occupation forces had bulldozed their house.

The first comment I got from Haya was the sort I would have expected. With a sickening laugh she scoffed, 'It's the first time I've ever heard "Butterfly" used as a code name! Ha ha ha ha!'

Desperately trying to control my temper, I said

irritably,

'That "ha ha ha ha" of yours doesn't suit a city girl!'

Trying to act as if she couldn't care less, Haya brushed her hair back with her fingertips and stuck her chest out as if to show me that she was more feminine and grown up than I was. Suddenly I saw the word 'SEPARATE' stamped across her face, and I got so tense, I could feel my body heating up.

Joining in on a more serious note, Mays said she agreed with Haya and, since she considered herself more politically savvy than me, tried to help me see why 'Butterfly' wouldn't work as a code name. But I refused to let them change my mind, and I didn't feel any obligation to reveal anything about my treasure chest. I felt as though this secret of mine made me special, and I was going to fight for it. In fact, it seemed like a matter of life or death—I rather liked the expression 'life or death'.

I also cherished the idea of dying for the sake of dreams and questions. *I was going to be a martyr, too, but stupid Haya and Mays would never understand that.*

I wished I could find somebody to share my dangerous secret with, somebody who could help me answer some of my questions. Not Tala, of course. I thought of Zaynab as a possibility, but she and I weren't that close. She liked to hole up with her own private concerns, which made me wonder: *does she have a treasure chest, too?*

I didn't really think so. The only thing that mattered to her was Omar, the man she loved and who'd been sentenced to life in prison. I stumbled on that information by accident, as I overheard her telling my mother about it when our paternal cousin Nasser, who was living in Saudi Arabia, asked for her hand in marriage, and my mother scolded her for falling in love. This was how I discovered that there was a connection between falling in love, honour and the Israeli occupation. The common denominator—to use a term we always heard from our Maths teacher Miss Ezzat—was that all three ended in disaster.

My mother was practically shouting, but she was trying to do it under her breath so that nobody else would hear her. Zaynab was mumbling that Omar had told her she was free to do whatever she thought was best. Then, her voice so strained and weepy that I felt sorry for her, she added, 'Don't worry, Mama. It won't affect my future. He told me we should break up, since he doesn't expect to get out of prison for a hundred years, and he doesn't want to tie me down.'

So this was poor Zaynab's secret. I couldn't believe it; I never would have wanted anything like this to happen to her. For a long time I'd been contemplating what I wanted to wear to her wedding, since she'd been planning to give me lots of her clothes when she got married. I was going to ask her for her black shoes and her red bag with the copper rings on it, as she was going to buy new things for her trousseau.

But what I thought about the most was the dress I was going to buy to wear at her wedding. It was low-cut, and once I'd stuffed the front with paper tissues, it would make me look as though I had a lot on top. I'd fantasised about going to the beauty salon with her to get my hair done and have my face made up, and how everybody would ask about me since I was the sister of the bride who got to sit near her and dance in front of her as she sat on the platform at the front of the wedding hall.

But now Zaynab was feeling awful, and I had to give up all these dreams, so I felt awful, too.

Why was marriage such a miserable affair in my country?

I thought about Salma and Rashid, and about Zaynab and her beloved Omar.

Then I added this question to my treasure chest too. Still holding the pen in my hand, I opened my diary and sat down cross-legged on the bed while Tala read the story of *The Fox and the Rooster* in a loud, irritating voice.

(4)
AM I REALLY THAT NAIVE?

Butterfly, go flying over the water like a seagull. I'd love to have a sea to float over. Palestine used to have two seas—the Mediterranean Sea and the Dead Sea—but both of them have been stolen. It also had a lake, Lake Tiberias, and that was stolen, too.

I shed a tear.

Butterfly, soar high like a plane. Unlike every other country in the world, mine doesn't have any planes, and it doesn't have an airport. All it has are crossings, checkpoints and bypass roads.

Another tear...

Butterfly, lap up my questions, feed on my dreams, clothe yourself with my ideas and spread out on my arms and my hair. Dream of my country without settlements so that Baba won't have to work for Gabby and Yuval anymore—not picking grapes, not picking dates, but planting a date palm of his own, a grapevine of his own, and an olive tree.

Another tear...

Butterfly, give my greetings to Saleh, to Uncle Yasin, to Bakr's legs, and to Grandpa Mubarak's crippled leg.

Another tear...

Butterfly, tell me: when will you and I be united in a single body so that we can go scatter dreams in the air and plant questions on the hilltops, where red anemones, daffodils and wild thyme can take root and grow?

Uncertainty...

Butterfly, go to sleep on my chest so that I can go to sleep in you, and I promise you we'll be born some day... but now, I feel drowsy.

There's hope!

'Ha!' sneered Haya. 'So now you've even started writing love poetry to your code name!'

She was up to her old, nasty trick of invading other people's privacy. She'd opened my bag and taken out my diary. Thank God she'd only started reading on the last page and hadn't seen what I'd written to 'N'—Nizar's first initial, which I used as a secret code so that if some nosy parker opened my bag without permission, she wouldn't know who I'd been writing to.

I decided not to react to Haya's provocation, since I was determined to keep my treasure chest a secret. Being the only one to know about it gave me a special, warm feeling, since the treasure chest was the only thing I had that was all my own, and I was afraid I might not be able to keep quiet about it if I started telling the story of the butterfly. Once I'd opened my mouth, the floodgates would open and I might end up telling Haya what I'd suppressed all this time, in case I ever needed to use it—namely, the rumour about her father and her grandfather.

It was one of the first days back at school and I'd been hoping to start off the new academic year without any upsets, especially since my summer had been so awful. Zaynab did get married, but she wasn't at all happy about it. Then she went to live in Saudi Arabia, and I cried my heart out. My face was covered with tears and snot when we said farewell on her wedding day, but I didn't bother to wipe it. It was a heart-wrenching, emotional scene. Even Baba cried and so did Grandma Amna.

As for me, I had the good fortune of witnessing these teary moments not just once, but twice. We drew straws to see who would go to Jordan with Baba and Zaynab to see her off at the airport and visit family, and for the first time ever, I drew the lucky straw. So when I saw Baba sobbing again in Jordan and everything being so miserable, I thought to myself, *Now I know why I won the draw: so that I wouldn't have to miss these depressing moments the second time around!*

When I returned home I didn't tell Tala, of

course, about those 'moving scenes', since she would have gloated over my bad luck. I was surprised to find that she'd put on weight while I was gone, even though I'd only been away a couple of weeks or so, and she said she had some important news to tell me, as though she'd had some amazing experience.

At my end, I made up most of the events I told her about—or, rather, I twisted and embellished the facts to fit my purposes. I painted her a glamorous picture of the airport and the planes, and I described how I'd helped Zaynab carry her luggage on board. In fact, though, we'd gone to the airport at night and the last thing I glimpsed there was Zaynab's hand as she waved to us with tears streaming down her face. I didn't see so much as a fly take off from the airport. I even suspected that Zaynab had just left in a car and that everyone had tricked me into thinking that she was getting onto a plane.

I wove a story for Tala about going into a haunted house in Jordan and playing with the ghosts there. Knowing what a chicken I am, afraid of my own shadow, she tried to act as if she believed me, but it was obvious from the expression on her face that she didn't. I also reported going out every day with my cousins Rana and Maysoun to walk around in the King Abdullah Gardens and how we'd stayed there until late in the evenings eating turmus and ice cream and having the time of our lives.

Unfortunately, the truth of the matter was that Rana and Maysoun were incredibly snobbish and I really couldn't stand them and I'm sure they didn't like me either. When we did go out, we were escorted by my uncle's wife Aunt Rabah, who made me sit still in one place on the pretext that she was afraid for my safety, while she let her daughters wander around wherever they wanted. I was in a virtual prison the whole time I was there.

This was something else I'd never admit to 'Miss Tala', no matter how many important things she told me had happened while I was away. I didn't tell Mays or Haya, either. Instead I invented exciting stories about everything. I wanted to give them the impression that I'd visited Heaven on earth even though, in fact, it had been a bit of a hell-hole.

The reality hit me when I got home: I'd really missed Palestine and my village. I'd missed Tala, and Haya, and Mays. I'd missed standing at the window every day and waiting for Nizar to pass by. I'd missed everything. Everything. Everything in Palestine felt precious, including our cat, Wadee.

When I got back I found out that our neighbour Abu Mansur had run him over early one morning when he was driving workers to Israel, and I felt awful. Tala took me to where Wadee was buried, and it made me think of a martyr's grave, especially since she'd planted a rose bush beside it. Then she made the first significant statement of her life, and that was when I realised that she'd grown up during my time away.

'I didn't get too upset when Wadee died,' she declared. 'After all, he's a martyr, since Abu Mansur ran over him on his way to work for the occupiers.' She tried to act as if she were fully convinced of every word she was saying and that she wasn't heartbroken. So she looked hilarious and miserable at the same time, and I didn't know whether to laugh or cry.

Visiting Jordan I realised that the children of Palestine were deprived of everything—they couldn't even play in the street. It reminded me of Jawhar, a boy from the village next to ours. He was martyred during *Eid Al Fitr* break while he was playing with a plastic shotgun in front of his house. A jeep had driven by and, thinking the boy was holding a real gun, an army sniper in the jeep pulled out his rifle and shot him dead.

'Children there can travel from city to city with their families in their cars or on buses, since there aren't any checkpoints. They don't have to carry their birth certificates with them everywhere they go to prove they're too young to have to show an ID. In Palestine, children have to prove they're children.'

When Miss Fayrouz asked us during the last ten minutes of our Social Studies class to talk about how we'd spent our summer holidays, Haya pointed to me as somebody who'd had a memorable summer, since I'd travelled outside Palestine. So I got up and rattled off all these observations as if I were giving a speech.

Trying to be shrewd, I mentioned some things and left out others that it wouldn't have been to my advantage to talk about. One of the things I couldn't bring myself to tell Haya was that I'd missed her when I was gone. I'd sensed that she was special, and not like my two supercilious cousins. Unlike my mother and everybody else, who were always scrutinising Haya's fingernails and her pencilled-in eyebrows, I felt bad for poor Haya. After all, she was going through the same things as the rest of us.

And Mays—or 'Dalal Mughrabi' as she liked to be called—seemed like a bona fide heroine to me. When she started leading school marches, chanting the whole way with a loudspeaker in her hand and her forehead covered with beads of sweat, I felt so lucky to have her as my friend. As for Nizar—'Abu Ammar', as he called himself—he was like no other boy in the whole world. His silvery grey sweater and his jet-black trousers were this magical 'something' that I'd hidden in my treasure chest. They were a question, a dream. He would hold the loudspeaker and chant, and so would Mays, one leading the boys and the other the girls. Then the boys and girls would come together at the intersection in a joint march. I wondered: *why is it that in other countries of the world, boys and girls don't seem to come out on marches the way they do in Palestine?*

As soon as I got home and settled down on my bed, I spent some time alone day-dreaming and added this question to my treasure chest. Then I shook the box out, letting the questions and dreams get mixed up with my clothes. As I sat there I imagined that I was suddenly enormously wealthy.

I dreamed I'd built an amusement park for myself, and for Tala, Munir, Salem, Maryam, Mays, Haya, Nizar, Abboud, Sawsan, al-Khansa, and all the children of Palestine. It had a haunted house where the 'ghosts' weren't occupiers. And, although

I'd only ever seen airplanes on television, I imagined myself getting bigger and bigger and bigger until I had wings the size of an airplane's.

By the time I got back from Jordan, I'd changed my mind about my future mother-in-law having to be from outside Palestine. In fact, I'd decided that the whole notion of leaving Palestine needed to be reconsidered.

Ideas like this scared and saddened me, since it felt like I was growing up, and becoming more and more like my mother. I even started watching some of her gloomy soap operas with her. The change surprised my mother, but it made her happy, too, since now she felt she had one daughter who'd matured and another one who'd grown up and got married. These were reasons to feel that things were going well with her family, which might give her one up on Uncle Mustafa's wife.

One morning early in the school year, Mays and I were sitting under the big umbrella in the courtyard to get away from the scorching September sun. She said to me, 'You aren't a blabbermouth like Haya, so I'm going to tell you a secret. But promise you won't tell anybody no matter what!'

'I promise!' I told her. 'I swear!'

As I said it, I suddenly felt hot, flushed and frightened, and my heart started pounding wildly in my chest. I had that sixth sense that people talk about.

Her face brightening shyly, Mays said,

'There's someone I like!'

My heart started pounding even harder.

'Really? Who is it? Tell me! Tell me!'

Then, with a smile I'll never forget, she said,

'Abu Ammar.'

I could feel my heart crashing. I realised Mays was using his code name in order to avoid having to mention his actual name, which we were all aware of. It was a name that came up a lot when we were talking about boys. I didn't understand everything Mays said, but I didn't want to ask her any more questions. If I talked about it, I would have blown my own secret, since I had a feeling I was going to pass out. It was then that I saw what a fool I was, even though other people described me as shrewd. All of a sudden I hated Mays and Nizar. I also despised the marches and the revolution, since I suspected that those were what had brought the two of them together. After all, they both marched in front, holding loudspeakers and leading the chants.

Afterwards Mays told me that Nizar had often commented to her, 'Your friend (meaning me) gives you all my news!' It was then I realised that when I had talked about Nizar to Mays, she had interpreted this as me relaying his news to her. In other words, when I tired myself out every day standing on tiptoe to see him, I'd been acting as a messenger between the two of them. And I hadn't had a clue! So then, I wondered, *am I really that naive?*

I wrote the question in big bold print and stuck it in my treasure chest. As I cried myself to sleep that night, Tala was arguing with Wadee in her dreams, and I realised that if I was going to sob out loud this way every night and Tala was going to have heart-to-hearts with a dead cat in her sleep, then it was a blessing that Zaynab had married and moved away, even if she was unhappy about it.

Actually, I really needed somebody to complain to—a shoulder to cry on. But, you see, nobody had time for me, and nobody would have understood me anyway. So I withdrew into myself. Taking some pleasure in feeling like a victim, I started thinking up tragic scenarios for myself.

In one of these scenarios I married a man I didn't love and then he divorced me. By the time we divorced we had a little girl and I would have to look after her by myself as a single parent from then on. I would need to go to work as a seamstress, since I hadn't finished my education.

I couldn't explain why I hadn't finished studying, since Baba would never have pulled me out of school or prevented me from going to college. It was just that I had to construct the story so that it ended with me working as a seamstress. And the reason I wanted it to end this way was that one of our neighbours, Su`ad—like nearly all the girls in the village who hadn't finished school—worked as a seamstress. Su`ad was always complaining about her work and I felt sorry for her.

Our family circumstances gave me plenty of reasons to feel down. Baba was jailed for some time and lost his job at the settlement after somebody slipped some herbicide into the water he used to irrigate the grapevines, and they died just like that. So our whole family was going through a really difficult time. But even though he'd lost his job, my father didn't forget to grieve over the grapevines, since he was the one who had planted them and nursed them to adulthood.

As for me, I hated grapes from then on. To this day I feel bitter whenever I eat them. And I resented the occupation more than ever. I loathed Haya, who didn't dare say a word about my father and everything that had happened to him when I was around. And I abhorred Mays, since she was enjoying a romance that I was convinced she'd stolen from me. I conveniently forgot about the fact that she had a brother in prison, and that another brother of hers hadn't enrolled at the university that term because he hadn't been able to save up enough for the fees. And the reason he hadn't been able to save up enough was that the Civil Administration hadn't issued him a work permit because, in the eyes of the occupation, his brother was a saboteur.

Gabby and Yuval had deserted my father. In fact, Yuval had accused him of being behind the culprit, if not actually being the culprit himself. As for Gabby, who received compensation for the dead grapevines from the Israeli Government, he totally ignored the years of devoted, loyal service my father had given to his farm.

I remarked to Baba matter-of-factly, 'Maybe somebody else had it all planned out from the start. Didn't you say that there's a struggle going on among the various farm owners on the settlement? Maybe Gabby did it himself so that he could collect the insurance money!'

Some of what I said made sense, but not all of it. My father chuckled and commented on what a shrewd analyst I'd become. But behind that good-natured smile of his, his face looked dejected and gaunt. His eyes were sunken, and the potbelly that Tala and I made fun of at times had shrunk quite a bit, while his hands bore the tell-tale signs of the hardship he'd endured on our stolen land.

What pained Baba the most was the way he was treated by Gabby and Yuval. One day I heard him lamenting bitterly to my mother, 'Can you believe how fast Gabby and Yuval have forgotten what a dedicated worker I was all those years?' Baba seemed defeated and helpless.

It was hard to imagine that he also had questions without answers. In any case, I reached out limply to catch the question and stuff it into the treasure chest with all the rest. I was going to announce to Haya, *'My father doesn't have a job anymore, and from now on he won't be allowed into the settlement or anywhere else in Israel while your father and your grandfather can come and go as they please. Are you happy now?'*

I was so dejected that I felt even older than the school principal, let alone that airhead Haya. I kept this question tucked away in my treasure chest and walked home by myself the way I did most days during that time.

It was raining hard, and the wind was thrusting me backwards and whipping my school uniform. I felt alone in the world with nothing to relate to but my dreams and my hidden questions.

(5)

AS LIGHT AS A BUTTERFLY

Rain was still falling outside the window, and Tala was eating nonstop. Scoffing at my warning that she was going to get fat as a sheep's tail, she put her thumbs behind her ears and fluttered her fingers at me with her tongue sticking out. She accused me of being jealous of her, since I was doomed to stay skinny as a rail and wouldn't ever be able to put on weight no matter how hard I tried.

Mama and Baba were lighting the traditional kanoun stove out in the yard. They brought some dried grapevine branches from the storage shed and lit them. Then, as the smoke dissipated and the fire settled into glowing embers, they brought the stove into the house. Despite everything, it felt good to have Baba spending more time with us at home and lighting a fire since we'd had to stop using the electric heater.

As Tala went on stuffing her face, I said, 'You've got to start eating less for another reason, too: Baba doesn't work on the settlement anymore.'

Unfazed, she replied, 'Baba has lots of sheep now, so if we get hungry, all we have to do is eat one of them.'

Shaking my head gloomily, I thought to myself: *Tala still thinks like a little girl!* She'd also reached the stage where we had to pile blankets on top of her and, sympathising with her plight, I'd make her pots of sage tea. She'd also sprouted a couple of lemon-sized mounds on her chest that looked to have a promising future, and I envied her.

However, what she hadn't thought through yet was that our sheep weren't for us to eat, and now that Baba had lost his job, they were all that our family had to live on. My father didn't know how to do any other kind of work, and Grandpa Mubarak didn't have any land to till, so he raised sheep on the outskirts of the village. Baba had been raised there in the camp, and according to Grandma Amna, he'd drunk milk from the ewes' teats.

'We won't go hungry,' Baba said, 'even if we have to go and live in tents like before. After all, the mountains are still bountiful.' As he spoke, he pointed to Mount Gerizim in the distance.

I was sure he wasn't serious, and that we weren't really going to go and live in tents again. Even so, I thought about what it would be like if we did have to, and wondered what Haya's reaction would be when she found out. Even though she'd always criticised my father's job, she was sure to gloat!

As I ruminated, I suddenly realised that I cared too much about Haya and her opinion. No matter what happened, she would always find something negative to say, and I wasn't going to get on a space shuttle and go wherever she thought I should. So I found myself developing a new attitude and I stopped caring so much about what other people thought. What mattered was for me to have my own opinion and for it to be based on conviction and common sense. It seemed like the best way to resolve the turmoil I'd been in of late. So I calmed down a bit, and as time went on, I got over my tendency to giggle at tense moments.

We could hear somebody calling over the village mosque's loudspeaker. It was still pelting down with rain outside, so the sound was muffled. I didn't pay much attention to it, since we were used to hearing calls like that. Just then, Tala came running in. She asked me if I knew or not.

'Of course I don't!' I snapped sarcastically. 'What do you mean?'

'There's a martyr in the village,' she announced breathlessly.

Her breath looked like the steam that comes out of a boiling tea-kettle. 'It's Abu Ammar, she added. 'Nizar, the boy who always used to walk past our house and would hold the loudspeaker during the school marches.

'Nizar is dead?............................Why??'

This question was in red ink. I stuffed it into my treasure chest and said nothing. It would be a long time before I could write anything again like my letters to Nizar, who stayed hidden in my diary in the opening phrase, 'Dear N...'

I was devastated—too dazed now to talk or ask questions.

I heard my mother stirring. She was looking for some warm clothes to go out in. I slipped on my coat and followed her. She didn't ask me where I was going the way she usually did. Neither did my father, who ran on ahead. As we walked through the pouring rain, people were running up and down the street. They were all going in different directions, but for the same reason: there was a martyr in the village.

Nizar lay on a wet slab of wood, wrapped in a Palestinian flag. It was Nizar, all right. I recognised his silvery grey sweater, his face, his eyes and the smile he always had whenever he saw me standing on tiptoe by the window. Nizar was smiling at me in spite of all the people around. And now everyone had come to say goodbye to him. His mother and sisters were crying. As his mother's tears fell onto his face, they told her, 'You're not supposed to cry over a martyr. Let him stay pure!'

So, I wondered, *do tears make a martyr impure?* And the question got wet in the rain.

Little Salem broke through the crowd and came up next to me. He kissed Nizar's cheek and murmured something to him very softly. He tried to smile like Nizar, but ended up crying like everybody else.

Hajja Safiya approached. Puffed up like a tent as usual, she was soaking wet. Her tears flowed like rain out of a winter sky, but without any theatrics. Mama supported her on her right arm to keep her from falling. Everybody was crying. But Nizar went on smiling at me even after they'd picked him up and taken him away.

Mays missed three days of school. When Haya asked after her, her sister said she had a bad cold. I couldn't do the same, since I didn't have a convincing excuse for my mother. I couldn't visit Mays, either, since if I had, I might have attracted somebody's attention. Even more importantly, I was just as distraught as Mays was. After all, Nizar was my secret beloved, and the fact that neither Mays nor even Nizar knew about it didn't change that. I didn't call her either, since my father couldn't pay the phone bill anymore. He'd said we could use his mobile phone for emergencies only, and none of us objected. After all, we didn't get calls from anybody but Zaynab in Saudi Arabia and my brother Abdullah at his university in Jerusalem, and the only other people we would call were Grandpa Mubarak and Grandma Amna.

Three days later, Mays, Haya and I walked home from school together without exchanging a word. Mays seemed to have wilted like the leaves that were falling from the trees along the sides of the road. Desolate both for her and for myself, I buried my secret in my heart, and in my treasure chest. Nizar had been, and still was, my most beautiful dream. Mays looked over at the cemetery, shedding quiet tears. My mind devoid of shrewd thoughts, I was a sky where clouds blew freely, and I felt a cotton-like whiteness covering my chest. I smiled through the sorrow, at rest. I was as light as a butterfly.

Tala went running after the sheep as I sat perched on a boulder at the top of the hill. I could see the settlement on the hill opposite. A little town with tidy houses, it looked as though it were made of colourful match-boxes that I could have set on fire with the strike of one little match. But it was getting bigger all the time.

I gazed down and saw Grandpa Mubarak's and Grandma Amna's tent. It looked tiny, like a star on the edge of the sky. Grandma Amna was coming and going as energetically as a little girl. Hadn't she been through what I was going through? It seemed to me as though she'd been born this way and would die this way. She hadn't changed since the time I was born.

She hadn't even changed when she got the news that Uncle Yasin had been martyred with the Palestinian armed resistance in Lebanon. She'd ululated, she'd sung and she'd twirled, making the wide sleeves of her dress billow out around her. And she hadn't let a single tear drop fall. When my mother told us the story, it seemed like something from another age, and we listened to it when we were little the way we would listen to a fairy tale.

As I sat on a soft carpet of red anemones, I wrote in the air: *Grandma Amna, will I ever be as resilient as you?*

Grandpa Mubarak was skipping after his sheep like an eighteen-year-old. Ever since his leg was wounded in the Six-Day War of 1967, he'd walked lopsided, and he'd been known ever since as al-a`raj, 'the one with the limp'. He loved the title, and wore it like a badge of honour. So when I wrote my name on test papers I started to add al-A`raj at the end, ignoring the last name on my birth certificate.

Which is more important: the name on my birth

certificate, or my grandfather's leg and the sacrifices made by the revolutionaries? I hid the question in my treasure chest. Nizar and Uncle Yasin were gone, and Grandpa Mubarak was still chasing his sheep with one and a half legs.

That evening I relaxed with Grandpa Mubarak and Grandma Amna in front of the tent. The lamp inside was lit and a full moon shone in the sky. Grandpa was listening to the news when suddenly he turned off the radio with an exasperated sigh and said, 'How long are our brothers going to be at each other's throats?' I thought to myself: *Ever since I can remember we've been leaving our real enemy in peace and going after each other!*

Echoing my own thoughts, he went on, his hand trembling as he rolled a cigarette with his home-grown tobacco, 'Why do we leave our real enemy in peace and go running after each other?'

Another question for the treasure chest.

Night fell, and everything was quiet. As morning approached, I woke up and started tossing and turning. Then I dozed off again, or nearly. The butterfly had started fidgeting in my chest. She heard the sheep's bleating and fluttered her wings, which were elongating and about to sprout under my arms. When they did, I turned into a glorious butterfly, surrounded by bursts of luminescent colour as more butterflies filled the tent.

I unfurled my wings and flew up and away with the shimmering butterfly cloud. Even the sheep romping in the pen came flying with us. When we reached a place over the city of boxes, we hovered there as I opened my traditional thobe at the top near my heart and scattered my questions and dreams, like matchsticks of all different sizes, colours and shapes.

When I woke up, the sun was laughing as she spread her hair over the hill. Sitting outside my grandparents' tent, I placed my hand on my heart, the place where I'd felt the butterfly getting bigger and stronger, and I knew I had what it took to go life's distance.

The sheep were scampering around me, and Grandpa Mubarak was darting after them like a boy. He called me by my favourite name, and I ran to join him.

GLOSSARY OF TERMS

Abu Ammar: literally 'Father of Ammar', this is the code name used by the late Yasser Arafat (1929-2004), who was chairman of the Palestine Liberation Organization (PLO) from 1969 until his death in 2004.

Al Jawwal and Cellcom: Palestinian and Israeli telecommunications companies, respectively.

Al-Khansa: a seventh-century Arab poetess born in Najd, located in the central region of the Arabian Peninsula. Al-Khansa was known for her elegiac odes, particularly those in which she mourned the deaths of her two brothers, Mu`awiya and Sakhr. Mu`awiya was killed in 612 CE by members of a rival tribe and Sakhr was killed while seeking to avenge Mu`awiya's death.

Dalal Mughrabi: a Palestinian militant who was a member of the Fatah faction of the PLO, and who took part in what is known as the 1978 Coastal Road massacre which resulted in the deaths of 38 Israeli civilians, including 13 children. Mughrabi and eight other militants were also killed in the course of the operation. She has been hailed as a martyr and a national hero among Palestinians, while in Israel she is seen as a terrorist.

Eid Al Adha: the 'feast of the sacrifice' is a Muslim celebration that falls on the 10th of Dhu al-Hijjah, the last month in the lunar based Islamic calendar.

Eid Al Fitr: the Muslim celebration that marks the end of Ramadan, the holy month of fasting.

Hajja: a woman who has completed the Haj, the pilgrimage to Mecca required by all Muslims. The term Hajja is used as a term of respect for an older woman.

Harisa: an Arab sweet made from semolina and topped with almonds and a rose-water flavoured syrup.

Intifada: the First Intifada was a Palestinian uprising against the Israeli occupation of the West Bank and Gaza that lasted from December 1987 to 1993. The Second Intifada, also known as the Aqsa Intifada, began when then-Israeli Prime Minister Ariel Sharon made a visit to the Aqsa Mosque (known to the Jews as Temple Mount), an act that was seen by Palestinians as highly provocative. There ensued a period of intensified Israeli-Palestinian violence that lasted from September 2000 until around 2005.

Martyr (noun, and verb 'to be martyred'): in the context of the Palestinian resistance against the Israeli occupation of Palestinian territory, a martyr is someone who dies or is killed while supporting the Palestinian cause.

Shami and Maghrebi: is a popular Arabic proverb.

Shami refers to people from Jordan, Lebanon, Palestine or Syria, whereas Maghrebi refers to people of The Maghreb (Algeria, Libya, Mauritania, Morocco and Tunisia). This proverb is used when very different people are willing to come together over a common cause.

Six Day War: also known as the 1967 Arab–Israeli War, this conflict was fought between 5 and 10 June, 1967 by Israel and the neighbouring states of Egypt, Jordan, and Syria. By the time a cease-fire was signed on 11 June 1967, Israel had occupied and annexed the Gaza Strip and the Sinai Peninsula (which had belonged to Egypt), Syria's Golan Heights, and the West Bank and East Jerusalem (until that time, part of Jordan).

Sunnah: the teachings, deeds and sayings of the Prophet Muhammed (peace and blessings be upon him), as well as various accounts of Muhammed's companions.

Thobe: an ankle-length garment, usually with long sleeves.

Turmus: the Arabic term for white lupine beans, which are prepared by soaking and salting. They are sold on the streets as a snack in numerous Arab countries.

Ululate: To utter a shrill, trilling sound as an expression of happiness.

Umm: Mother. Traditionally people address a married woman with a son as 'the mother of ...'

With irony and poignant teenage idealism, Butterfly draws us into her world of adult hypocrisy, sibling rivalries, girlfriends' power plays, unrequited love....not to mention the political tension of life under occupation. As she observes her fragile environment with all its conflicts, Butterfly is compelled to question everything around her.

Is her father a collaborator for the occupiers? Will Nizar ever give her the sign she's waiting for? How will her friendship with the activist Mays and the airhead Haya survive the unpredictable storms ahead? And why is 'honour' such a dangerous word, anyway?

'Full of humour, brave and honest, Code Name: Butterfly is by far the best young adult novel from the Arab world I've ever read.'
Susanne Abou Ghaida, PhD candidate, University of Glasgow, previously with the Anna Lindh Foundation

'A beautiful, astounding book that daringly, yet seamlessly blends the dreamy world of adolescence with the tough questions it brings. Code Name: Butterfly speaks with intelligence, wit and irony about the injustices and implications of occupation.'
Jehan Helou, Chairman, The International Board on Books for Young People – Palestine Chapter

When she was a little girl, Ahlam Bsharat dreamed of becoming a singer, a painter, a fashion designer, or a farmer like her mother. But all along she was on her way to becoming an author. In writing she found the way to make all her dreams come true.

ISBN 978-1-911107-02-6

9 781911 107026 >

Neem Tree
PRESS

£10.48
info@neemtreepress.com

Milton Keynes UK
Ingram Content Group UK Ltd.
UKHW022227130624
444044UK00006BA/130